by Adam Beechen
based on the teleplay by Gene Grillo
illustrated by Mark Marderosian

Ready-to-Read

Simon Spotlight/Nickelodeon

New York   London   Toronto   Sydney   Singapore

Based on the TV series *The Adventures of Jimmy Neutron, Boy Genius*™
as seen on Nickelodeon®

SIMON SPOTLIGHT
An imprint of Simon & Schuster Children's Publishing Division
1230 Avenue of the Americas
New York, New York 10020

Manufactured in the United States of America

4 6 8 10 9 7 5 3

Library of Congress Cataloging-in-Publication Data
Beechen, Adam.
Jimmy on ice / by Adam Beechen ; illustrated by Mark Marderosian.—
1st ed.
p. cm. — (Ready-to-read ; #2)
Based on the TV series The adventures of Jimmy Neutron, boy genius.
Summary: When the summer sun becomes too hot for Jimmy and his friends,
Jimmy the boy genius makes it snow in Retroville, but then finds there is
a new problem to solve.
ISBN 0-689-85294-0
[1. Sun—Fiction. 2. Science fiction.] I. Marderosian, Mark, ill.
II.Title. III. Series.
PZ7.B383 Ji 2003
[E]—dc21
2002006303

Jimmy Neutron and his friends
Carl and Sheen played
in Jimmy's backyard
under the hot summer sun.
"Aargh!" Sheen cried.
"Ultra Lord can't take this heat!"
"Neither can I," said Jimmy. "We
need to cool off."

"Cindy, can we come over
   and play in your pool?" Jimmy asked.
"Sure," said Cindy, smiling at Libby.
"But first you have to admit
   that girls are better than boys!"

Carl and Sheen nodded,
eagerly eyeing the pool.
But Jimmy said, "No way!
I will fix the weather myself.
How hard could it be?"

"I am getting scorched, I should put on some more sunblock," said Carl.

"Sunblock?! Carl, you are a genius!" Jimmy cried.

"I am?" Carl asked.

"I am making Carl's sunblock
   nine hundred times more powerful,"
   said Jimmy. "It will shield
   all of Retroville!"
Goddard barked with concern.
"Do not worry, boy," Jimmy said.
"What could go wrong?"

Jimmy loaded the sunblock into a
missile and launched it from his roof.
"There it goes!" he shouted
as it soared toward the sun.
Jimmy's father looked up
from his lawn chair.

"All this heat is making me
woozy," he said.
"I thought I just saw a missile
fly out of my house!"
Seconds later, the missile exploded,
and a huge cloud of sunblock
covered the sun.

"Jimmy, you did it!" Carl shouted
as the snowflakes started to fall.
"Yes, I did!" Jimmy said proudly.

All over Retroville, people
came out of their houses
and looked up at the sky.
They put away their bathing suits
and put on their snowsuits.

Everyone spent the rest of the day throwing snowballs, building snowmen, sledding, ice-skating, and making snow angels.

That night, Jimmy looked out from
his window and admired the snow.
"For once, everything turned out
perfectly," he said, smiling.

Jimmy's room was transformed
into an icicle cavern overnight.
"Leapin' leptons!" Jimmy cried,
his eyes widening in horror.
"I think I made a tiny error!"

Jimmy went to his lab and grabbed
Carl's sunblock bottle.
"'DO NOT MAKE 900 TIMES STRONGER
THAN NORMAL,'" he read. "'COULD CAUSE
SECOND ICE AGE.' Oh, no!"

"J-J-James Isaac N-N-Neutron!"
called Jimmy's mother, her
teeth chattering.
"W-Whatever you d-did, Jimmy,
you have t-to undo," said his
father, shivering.
"Do not worry," Jimmy replied.
"I will fix everything!"

At school Jimmy's classmates
formed a circle around him.
"Get him!" they shouted.
"He turned Retroville into
a freezing glacier!"
"Hurry, Goddard!" Jimmy shouted.
"Snow-ski mode!"

Goddard turned into a snowmobile,
and they raced away from school
with an angry mob chasing them.
"The cold weather has turned them into
cave people," Jimmy said with a gasp.

Jimmy and Goddard sped
over the frozen streets.
They turned a corner and saw Carl
standing in front of a big igloo.
"Hi, guys," he said. "Come inside!"

"Wow," Jimmy said. "What's
    all this for?"
"I am getting ready to sleep
    through the winter," Carl told him.
"By the time it's over,
    my sunburn will be gone!"

Jimmy paused. "Sunburn?
Weren't you wearing sunblock?"
"I must have sweated it off,"
Carl replied, shrugging.
"I am a good sweater."
"That's it!" shouted Jimmy.
"Sunblock dissolves in water!"

Jimmy ran all over Retroville
looking for water. Unfortunately,
the hydrants were frozen,
Cindy's pool had turned to ice,
and the water pipes didn't work.

Jimmy thought hard as Carl's words echoed in his head: *I am a good sweater . . . sweater . . . sweater. . . .* Jimmy's mind went to work.

"Brain blast!" he shouted.
"Sweat doesn't freeze as fast as
water. All I need is a lot of sweat,
and then I can melt the sunblock!"

Soon Carl and Sheen were
at Jimmy's house doing
jumping jacks and sweating
in front of a roaring fire.

"Once that can is filled
with your sweat, I will shoot it
at the cloud of sunblock,"
Jimmy explained.
"That should end the winter!"

Jimmy ran outside and aimed the nozzle at the sun. Everyone watched as he pressed down on the sprayer.

"Sweat away!" he yelled.
"Eeew," everyone groaned, holding
their noses at the awful smell!

27

At first nothing happened.
Then the sun broke through
the sunblock cloud,
the temperature rose,
and the snow started to melt.
"Hooray!" everyone cheered.

Retroville's lawns turned green again. Icicles fell from the roofs. And the ice in Cindy's pool melted. "That's our genius!" said Jimmy's parents, hugging him.

"You saved us all
  with my stinky sweat," Carl said.
"How can I thank you?"
"That's easy," Jimmy told his friend.
"Take a shower!"